#
Bertha

**Written by**
**CECELIA MARGULES**

**Illustrated by**
**KAYA BEALE**

Written by Cecelia Margules
Written & edited by Adam Margules
Adapted by Elliot Allen & Adam Cole

Published in association with Bear With Us Productions

ISBN 978-1-7367434-0-9

Dedicated to my mother, whose
imagination continues to inspire me.
She wrote the story, I put it out to the world.

Debby's bedroom is a mess! Clothes and toys piled to heights seemingly taller than a kid could even reach. It's dark from the piles of junk blocking light from coming through the windows. The walls are covered in music posters featuring a certain Pop Punk band (the child is clearly a big fan). The only piece of decor in the room that gives it some semblance of order is an empty white, vase that sits on a desk. There is a human shaped lump scampering under the piles of clothes on the floor.

"DEBBBBBBY! Clean up your room!" Mom shouts

The lump stops moving. From under the piles of clothes on the floor emerges DEBBY, a fiesty, independent, eleven year old girl, clever, sometimes too much for her own good, dressed in yellow overalls and holding up a vinyl record from the same band featured on the posters above.

"But Ma!" Debby moans.

"Don't 'but ma!' me." Mom snaps, "I've been asking you to clean it up now for two weeks, but it still looks like a pig sty in there! And you know the deal, you won't get those concert tickets you've been asking for until your room is spic and span."

"But ma, they're my favorite band! And my room isn't even a mess. Everything is exactly where it's supposed to be. Look! I just found my favorite record!"

Debby looks at the record in her hand.

"OOOF, that's not right" Debby continued quietly to herself.

"You heard me Debby," Mom said sternly; "first you clean-up your room, then you get the tickets!

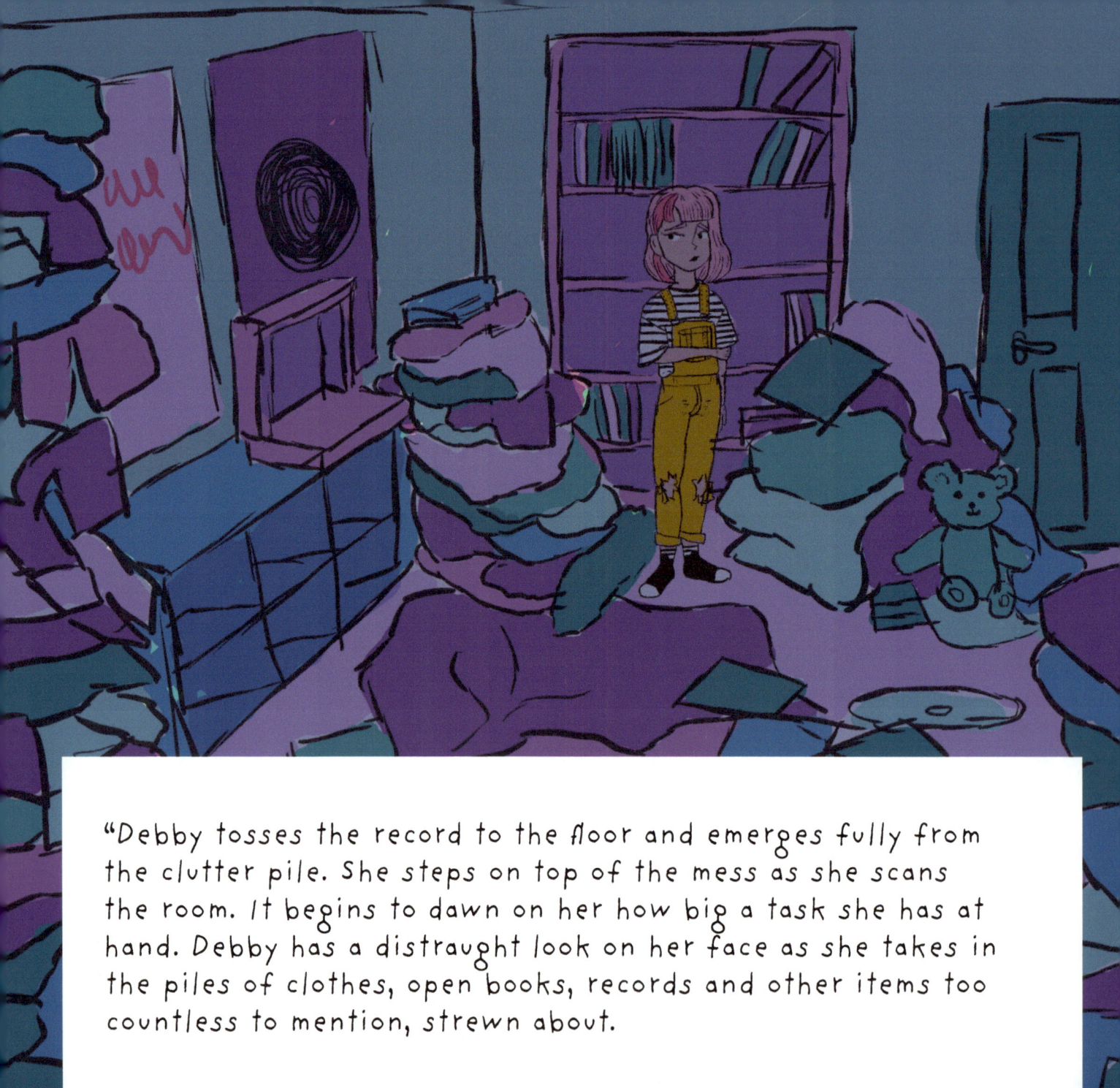

"Debby tosses the record to the floor and emerges fully from the clutter pile. She steps on top of the mess as she scans the room. It begins to dawn on her how big a task she has at hand. Debby has a distraught look on her face as she takes in the piles of clothes, open books, records and other items too countless to mention, strewn about.

Debby picks up an article of clothing and tries to fold it, but she can't get it right. She groans and throws the clothes back on the floor. Standing next to her desk frustrated, she folds her arms, looks at the vase and kicks the foot of the desk. The vase wobbles, tips over, and shatters. Debby throws her arms to her side in fists and fumes. She turns her back to the mess, gets into bed, shuts the light and clutches her blanket as she uneasily tries to fall asleep.

Morning comes and Debby is still in bed, a mirror of where she was at the beginning of the previous day. Suddenly, her eyes open wide with shock! Her room is immaculately clean: her clothes have been folded and put back in her closet, her records neatly returned to where they belong, her desk arranged beautifully.

On it lies the vase, now overflowing with a brilliant bouquet of flowers. Behind them the springtime sun shines, filling the room with sunlight. Debby's shocked expression clicks into an ecstatic smile and she leaps out of the covers onto her bed. She puts her hands to the sky while singing and dancing!

"YEE!" cheers Debby with joy, "I got my rooooom clean! I got my roooom clean!"

Debby's shocked expression clicks into an ecstatic smile and she leaps out of the covers onto her bed. She puts her hands to the sky while singing and dancing!

"YEE!" cheers Debby with joy, "I got my rooooom clean! I got my roooom clean!"
There's a KNOCK on the door. Debby stops jumping and looks towards the door.

Mom says; "I'm so proud of you Debby" and shuts the door behind her. Debby's eyes move from the door back to the tickets and her smile fades to a guilty frown.

Debby puts the tickets aside; she doesn't want to look at them anymore. Her eyes move towards the bouquet of flowers illuminated by the sunlight. She takes a step forward, buries her head in the bouquet, takes a deep breadth and lets out a sigh of relief.

"Mmmm..." Debby can get used to this new room!

It's the middle of the night and debby is tossing and turning in bed. She is not sleeping well.

A quiet voice says; "Darling..."

Debbie, remains asleep continuing to toss and turn, mumbling some nonsense in her restlessness

"Darling..." the voice says slightly louder.

Debbie remains unfazed.

"DARLING...!!"

Debbie's eyes jump open and she instantly sits up in bed. She awakens to see before her, a homely lady dressed in a simple maids outfit. Her silver hair kept in place with a bonnet. She is donning large spectacles which magnify her eyes and a messy apron over her floral dress. A crossover of Mrs. Doubtfire and Mary Poppins.

"Oh darling sweetie, did I wake you?" said the stranger coyly, "I thought I was being as mum as a field mouse.

Debbie blinked a few times

"Who are you?...Am I dreaming?"

The stranger begins to walk around, taking mental notes of the mess in the room.

"Oh darling", chuckled the stranger, "how would I know if you're dreaming? I can barely tell when I'm dreaming myself. And if you ask me, who cares!? People these days always expect the simplest answer to things...". The stranger let out a sigh. "But c'est la vie.

Debbie didn't respond and just looked at the confusing sight before her.

"The name's Bertha sweetie! And oh my is it a dreadful mess in here, even worse than the rumors. You see, I work for an agency, "Perfect House""

"Huh? Agency?! What agency? What are you doing here?" Debby started.

"I'm here to see if the rumors were true, darling. Turns out this place truly is as dreadful as they said. You see, darling, your room is the talk of the town, and we at Perfect House Agency could never let a situation like this go on. Something just had to be done, sweetie. And I am the best in the business! At your service!"

Bertha extends her arms as she curtsies, but as she bows down, she knocks over a pencil box which falls to the floor.

"Oh...oh dear", Bertha said. "Don't worry about that darling, I'll clean that right up..."

Bertha pushes the pencils on the floor out of the way with the tip of her toe.

Bertha continued "You see I'm a problem solver. Here's my card darling."

Bertha hands Debby a business card that only includes her name, the agency title and is blank white besides that. Debby holds the business card in both her hands. Her cunning smile grows into a mischievous smirk -- she thinks this could be her way out.

"Darling, I promise I'll have this place spick and span in 3. 2." SNAP!

One week later. Debby is asleep, her room is looking a bit disheveled; she has already reverted to her bad habits. Some clothes remain on the floor and several records are out of place. Suddenly, a heap full of clothes fall on Debby's head. She jolts up to see Bertha cleaning her room once again.

"Huh! Bertha? You're back?! What are you doing here?"

"Back?! Darling, I've been here every night this week, making sure your room stays spic and span", says Bertha. "You're an awfully messy little girl, you know Debby."

Bertha gives a playful wink. "Who do you think has been cleaning your room every night?

"Oh Bertha, I knew it was you!

"Yes, darling, of course it was me. But today is my final day on the job. Alas darling, it is time for me to leave."

"Oh no, Bertha! Don't leave just yet. I love you!"
Cries Debby.

"But my job here is done, darling; Perfect House agency
has many other clients I must attend to. Now it's your
turn to continue on your own. Good luck, Debby!"

"Ok, Bertha! I won't let you down!" Debby shouts.

It's the middle of the afternoon and Debby is in her room. She walks up to her neatly organized record collection, easily pulls out the one she was looking for and puts it in the record player. She sits at her desk and starts doodling and happily bobbing her head.

Unfortunately, this happy situation does not last for long. Gradually the mess in her room begins to accumulate once again. Piles of clothes begin to rise up, records fall out of their organized spots and the flowers on her desk beside her begin to wilt.

Even the weather begins to change from beautiful sunny springtime to shorter, darker rainier days.

Debby's attitude mirrors the changing weather. From gleeful and happy, her energy softens, and her eyes start to dim.

Debby is asleep at her desk in a room that was just as messy as before.

Then suddenly, SNAP!

It's the morning and Debby is back in bed. She wakes up with a jolt. She sees a lump moving around the mess of her clothes. Out pops Bertha.

"Oh darling dear, don't mind me" says Bertha cheerfully. I just came back to pick up some very important documents I left behind, but I can't for the life of me find them. But golly roger, darling. It's an absolute pig sty in here. What happened?!"

"I...I don't know" says Debby, holding back tears.

Bertha looks at Debby and then moves to the now dead flowers.

"Oh dear", says Bertha sadly.

Bertha removes her sunglasses and puts them down. She walks towards the bed and sits beside Debby. She tenderly touches her face.

"Don't worry darling", Bertha continued gently. "I know what happened here. It's not your fault. You see, I didn't actually leave a Perfect House...I broke my promise.

Debby's tearful eyes met Bertha's

"Everything around me just fell apart...Bertha, you always seem so...magical. How do you do it?"

"There is no magic", chortled Bertha! "The secret is to start one step at a time. Here let me show you. It's time to pick things up darling!

Bertha begins folding clothes as Debby watches her.

"If you have a task and don't know where to start", continued Bertha with a light tune "And you feel like your world is falling apart, Too scary, too hard; you might want to quit, But no! The answer is to start bit by-bit!"
Then Bertha gives debby a stern stare. "Come along now, darling! Just follow me."

(Upbeat music kicks in as the mood in the room suddenly changes.)

Debby gets up and starts mimicing Bertha. Bertha and Debby whisk around the room in a playful mood, having fun cleaning up. Bertha starts to dance a bit to the rhythm, as she moves junk around and Debby follows suit.

Soon they are both fully dancing as they clean up Debby's room. They put on a fashion show as they move the clothes from the floor to the closet. Bertha frisbees records to Debby as she puts them into their correct spot.

Bertha and Debby both have brooms and they spiritedly sweep together in unison. As Debby becomes more spirited, Bertha takes a step back and exclaims;

"Yes, darling! You're a natural! You're a star! You're a queen! Yes, darling! Yes, that's it!..." Debby doesn't notice Bertha beginning to fade away, leaving Debby continuing to clean with a smile on her face.

She continues to sing to herself as she cleans when there is a sudden KNOCK on the door

Mom Yells; "Everything ok in there?"

Debby, not noticing her mom, continues to clean and dance. The door CREAKS open and Mom walks in.

"Oh Dee! it looks amazing in here!" Says Mom proudly.

Debby smiles with glee.

"I am so proud of you, darling!" Mom continued.

Debby, still sweeping, turns her head back to her mom. "Thanks mom, I learned from the best".

"Learned what, honey?" Mom asked.

Debby's face transcends into a broad  smile.

"If you have a task and don't know where to start, And you feel like your world is falling apart, Too scary, too hard; you might want to quit, But no! The answer is to start bit by-bit!" sings Debby.

www.ingramcontent.com/pod-product-compliance
Lightning Source LLC
Chambersburg PA
CBHW041538240626
47164CB00002B/55